GHAZALA NAAZ

First Published in January 2022

ISBN: 978-93-93388-32-2

BLUEROSE PUBLISHERS

www.bluerosepublishers.com
info@bluerosepublishers.com
+91 8882 898 898

Cover Design:
Aveek

Typographic Design:
Rohit

Distributed by: BlueRose, Amazon, Flipkart

Dedicated to

My Mom, Nuzhat

Who made me into what I am today,

And

My daughter, Saima

Who is everything that I ever wanted to be.

Contents

A Pebble

The dark easterly clouds gathering overhead were a welcome relief from the suffocating heat of the day. Bhagwanti put aside the rice that she was picking clean for the evening meal, stretched, and headed outside her cramped hutment to enjoy the cool, moist pre-monsoon breeze. The space outside her house had a large Banyan tree and she tried to keep the ground under it swept and watered in the dry weather. Right now, however, many leaves and twigs littered the area because of the strong, easterly wind. It was almost dusk and smoke from the evening cooking was billowing out of several houses in the vicinity. The paddy in the fields, stretching unbroken on all sides, swayed, and danced to the tune of the wind. Bhagwanti felt her spirits lifting and the weight of her singleness blowing away as she stood looking towards the grey clouds filling up the sky. Her weathered face bore a smile as she turned towards a voice beckoning her.

"Tai...Tai" * shouted a young boy of about twelve as he ran towards her with his windswept hair and shirt fluttering around him. Bhagwanti recognized him immediately.

"What Bholu? Is Vrinda Chachi* already in labour?" She questioned.

"Hurry Tai. Chhota-chacha* asked me to fetch you immediately. Chachi is in great pain." He panted.

As the only midwife in the village, Bhagwanti was used to handling such emergencies. She scurried inside, covered the fire to smother it, put away the rice she was going to cook in an earthen pot, picked up the bag containing the tools of her trade which had belonged to her mother, wore her Bata flip flops, and ran a comb through her oiled hair. She was ready.

'Bholu, hold this', she said to the boy as she handed him her trade bag and bolted her door on the outside.

Then the boy and the fifty-year-old woman, wearing a faded pink and green sari, which had seen better days, hurriedly made their way through the meandering dirt path in between the paddy fields.

The predominant thought in Bhagwanti's mind was, "Let this be a boy Prabhu* – for Vrinda and for my sake."

Outside the house, which they reached in about fifteen minutes, the men sat waiting in the open-air courtyard, sharing a hookah. Bhagwanti adjusted her pallu* over her head, looked in their direction, and held the palms of her hand together in greeting. The village Sarpanch, who was also the grand-father-to-be, spoke out to her-

"Pranam* dai*. Hurry and get down to business - make us happy and we'll make you happy."

The midwife knew what he wanted – what all of them wanted, every time. A boy.

She gave a toothy grin, picked her sari up to her ankle, and stepped over the threshold into the inner courtyard.

She could hear Vrinda groaning in pain from the bedroom. This was one of the rare pucca houses in the village. Instead of heading to that room, Bhagwanti headed for the kitchen to her left. She knew the layout of the house well. She still remembered assisting her mother in the birth of both the Sarpanch's sons. The kitchen was empty. She looked around for Bholu, but he too had deserted her after handing her the bag once they had reached the door. She cursed him as she bent and rummaged through the pots and pans for a large vessel that could be filled with water. She then put it on a kerosene stove to heat. That done she finally headed to her patient.

It was a typical scene from a birthing room in the village. The patient was on the bed writhing in pain. Her mother-in-law, seated on a chair on one side, looked on as her younger daughter-in-law, barely out of her teens herself, tried to help Vrinda, by stroking her head. The house help, Jugini, was standing at the foot of the bed, wringing her hands helplessly. Bhagwanti immediately took command.

Jugini was sent off to the kitchen to fetch the hot water. The young daughter-in-law was asked to get clean cloth which she ran off to bring, relieved. Bhagwanti herself started to reassure her patient as she busied herself in checking the baby's head and its position. Vrinda had a slim structure, and this was her first time. The labour wasn't going to be easy, Bhagwanti knew. She had spent all her life assisting births and had learnt her craft well at her mother's side. She prepared herself for a long vigil.

As Bhagwanti assisted the young mother-to-be in pushing the baby out, women from adjoining homes walked in and out of the room. The birth of the child was a community affair, and everyone wanted a part in the festivity. A lone, naked light bulb lit the room. Electricity was a recent luxury in the village. Bhagwanti had set up an old sari on bamboo support as a cover around the woman, to protect her from prying eyes. No man was allowed into this room. Not even the husband. Birthing was an all-female affair. And there were no boundaries among women. However, the midwife wanted to protect the privacy of her patient. She didn't like her to be too exposed.

The struggle continued late into the night, with thunder and lightning adding a befitting backdrop. Bhagwanti wasn't very young herself and she felt tired by all the effort and anxiety. Her patient was also exhausted by the pain and the pushing. But she continued to talk and persuade.

"Just a little more bahu*. It's almost done."

"I'll die!" Her patient groaned in response.

"Don't be silly. Nothing will happen to you," retorted Bhagwanti, but she wasn't so sure in her heart. This one was proving to be difficult. She prayed for it to be over soon.

It was much after midnight, just before the darkest hour, that an infant's cry was heard in the Sarpanch's house. But the midwife was stunned by what she held in her hands. Smeared in blood, it was a girl. All that struggle only to end in this, she thought. The family would be so displeased. This meant her fee would be curtailed and there would be no extra gifts for her. A pall, a sense of gloom, filled the room as she handed the new-born baby to her grandmother. The disappointed woman reluctantly took the warm bundle and went outside. Bhagwanti busied herself in cleaning up the new mother who was prostrate on the bed, in a semi-conscious state, too exhausted to care.

In a little while, she heard someone call her from the outside. She looked at the sleeping woman and stepped out into the dark courtyard. The village crowd had dissipated. The Sarpanch was standing alone, holding the bundle in his hand. He gave it to her along with a wad of currency notes. She knew what he wanted. All he said was,

"Make it quick and easy."

Bhagwanti walked out with her little load. It had rained heavily, and the ground was wet. She knew what she had to look for. This wasn't the first time for her.

In the pitch dark, as her eyes adjusted, she bent and started looking around. Soon she found it. The perfect pebble – small and round. She checked to see if there was anyone around. Then, expertly, she pushed the pebble down the infant's windpipe.

The little one spluttered, choked, and was silenced forever.

Bhagwanti handed the dead package back to the Sarpanch. His wife started wailing. It was a loud wail proclaiming death to everyone in the neighbourhood. Bhagwanti quickly gathered her belongings before the sleeping woman woke up and made her way back towards her own hut.

The distant sky had started to light up a little, but the warm glow was not reflected in Bhagwanti's heart. It was a dark and cold place, pregnant with murky secrets.

GLOSSARY

Tai - Aunt

Chachi – Aunt

Chhota-chacha – Father's younger brother

Dai – a midwife

Prabhu – God

Pallu – a part of the sari which is used as a head cover

Pranam – greeting

Bahu – daughter-in-law

Blurred Vision

Greedily, I eyed the packet of cream biscuits. How I had craved to eat one and now I was going to get a whole pack - all to myself. I could not believe my luck! My whole being was focused on the gift in Baba's* hand. He had held it up close to me and had promised to let me eat all of it if I was a good girl. He held my hand as we crossed the road to get to the Bus Stand. Amma* was also with us but she was lagging far behind. She didn't seem her usual hyper self today. She was neither showing irritation with Baba nor scolding me. Probably, what the Doctor had said about my eyes was bothering her. I couldn't care less. I had never known any better. My eyesight had been weak from as far back as I could remember.

On the construction site where my parents worked, I often got hurt because of my inability to see things at a distance. But I had learnt to bear silently, for drawing attention to my pain usually invited angry lashings from my mother. Her helplessness, anxiety, frustration was all directed against my poor vision. She would use her fists, elbows, feet to rain blows on me and then end up wailing and cursing her fate. So, I had, early in life, made peace with a white haze and blurred images. That was my world.

I turned to look at my mother who was still trailing behind. If I focused with concentration, I could see her struggling to keep up, with her protruding belly, in her pink and gold sari. Deliberately, I let go of Baba's hand and slowed down so that she could catch up with us. I didn't want her lost in the sea of faces around us. This was a precious moment for me. Amma, Baba, and I were visiting the big city together for the first time. A rare occurrence indeed…

I clearly remembered the sequence of events that had led to this trip. The site engineer, a young, fair man called Vikas sahib, had been inspecting the construction work when some men came to shoo away the children playing on the sand heaps there. All the kids scampered away, but I tripped on a brick and lay sprawled near Vikas sahib's feet. As I tried to pick myself up, he stooped to give me a hand and said, not unkindly,

"Careful there! What's your name?"

The man held in awe by all the adults around, talking to me? Dumbstruck, I just stared back.

"You don't have a name?" There was a smile in his voice as he asked me again.

A woman worker, hanging nearby, nudged me. "Why don't you tell the Sahib your name?"

"Moni," I whispered shyly.

"Who is your father?" That was the next question fired at me.

"Rahim…Muhammed Rahim," I stammered.

By now several onlookers had gathered around to see what was happening. The young engineer casually asked one of the workers,

"Is there some problem with this child's eyes?"

My father had been alerted by now and he arrived on the scene, panting and anxious.

"Yes, Sahib ji*, she can barely see," he piped in and then added, "since her birth."

"Rahim?" The Sahib confirmed before questioning, "Have you shown her to a doctor?"

Baba meekly folded his hands and said, "No Sa'ab, we barely manage our meals. Where is the money for a doctor's fee?"

"So, you'll let her be like this?" reprimanded the Sahib, showing concern. How old is she?"

"Almost four Sahib," Baba responded.

"How will she earn her living? Who will marry her? You must get her treated." The Sahib countered.

"We too worry Sahib, but what can we do," replied Baba.

Not finding anything interesting happening, the crowd which had been collectively staring, began to scatter.

"When the Chairman Sa'ab visits," said the Sahib, "I'll recommend your child's case to him. There is an eye specialist who holds a free clinic, once a week, near the bus stand, in the city. If the Bada Sa'ab* talks to him, he will treat Moni, free of cost."

Baba bowed his head in gratefulness and told me gruffly, "touch the Sahib's feet, he is so kind."

When I did not move from my place, overawed as I was, he roughly pulled me up and almost pushed me to the ground. I quickly bent to touch the revered feet. Annoyed by the fuss, Sahib raised his voice and barked,

"Come on, come on everyone, get to work you lazy bums! One little reason is enough to hang about and waste time." Those still standing and staring also started to move away.

I have a special reason for remembering this conversation in detail. Baba repeated it to Amma, word for word, in our makeshift tenement that evening, while she cooked rotis for him. That I was a burden on my parents had been drilled into me time and again by my mother. I had an older sister and a younger brother and Amma's swollen belly was an indication that another mouth was on its way. She was worn and thin and looked much older than her age. My stumbling and knocking things about in the small hut exasperated her. She would hit me or pull my hair every time.

Baba and Amma that night, had hope in their voices. They discussed the happy possibility of a cure that would relieve them of a heavy burden. I felt light in my heart too. The atmosphere inside the hut was warm and cosy as I drifted off to sleep in my corner on the floor.

A couple of days later, Amma shook me awake and asked me to quickly wash and change. She handed me the only clean frock that I had, brought from a second-hand vendor, the previous Eid. I stumbled out and made my way to the hand pump in the common washing area. The place was not very crowded as it was still early. The sun had just started to rise. As I washed my hands and feet in the cold water, I felt a rising anxiety inside of me. What will the doctor do? I had never really seen one before. Medicines I had taken earlier but injections were scary. I had gathered from the conversations of the adults around me that a time had been fixed for me, with the eye doctor, by the owner of the site. I was excited to be paid so much attention. This was the first time that I was going to the city with Baba and Amma. I had heard from some of the other children how big and grand it was.

After changing into my blue frock, I picked up a broken comb, lying in a tin box in the hut, to unknot my hair. Amma took the comb and quickly ran it through my hair and plaited it. She did this only on special occasions. She was dressed and ready. Rarely did she get an opportunity to go out. Baba, looking important in his much washed and frayed t-shirt and pants, commanded us to follow him.

The early morning sun, the thin mist of dawn, and my state of excitement – all combined to create a dream-like atmosphere, as we stepped out on the road to make our way to the bus stop. Baba had a paper in his hand, given to him by the Sahib, which had the bus number which we were to take to the city, and the address written on it. This bus went through the street which had the Doctor's clinic. As he looked for the right bus, I clung to Amma's Sari. I tried to focus, but my vision was confined to a small circular area and the rest was a blurred white haze. The deafening noise of the traffic near the bus stop and the shoving and pushing of people as they tried to make their way into the different buses, was scary. I was used to living in the isolated harbours of the construction sites, either playing or helping Amma with her chores. We rarely came to the busier parts of the town.

I remembered seeing clearer when I was younger. My problem was growing with me. The prospect of seeing better was exciting. But right then I just wanted to turn around and go back to the corner of the shelter and huddle with my sister and brother, who were still sleeping. After some jostling, we got on our bus. Amma and I squeezed into a seat with two other ladies. I could smell the jasmine in the hair of one of them. It was a heavenly fragrance. Baba stood deferentially among educated people travelling to their offices. I tried to look and make sense of all the sights outside the window, but it was mostly a coloured haze. I got tired after a little while. The whiff of the jasmine mixed with the exhaust fumes and the sweaty bodies was sickening. I rested my head against the seat in front and closed my eyes.

When I had almost dozed off, I was brusquely awakened by my mother as our stop was approaching. We got off the bus as it stopped and then hastily crossed the road. A car came close to hitting us and screeched to a halt. The driver shouted at us rudely,

"You rustics! Look where you're going. Don't die under my car!"

Baba hurriedly got us out of the way and then showed the paper with the address on it to an auto-rickshaw driver who pointed out a building to us. Baba headed towards it with us in tow. I was very confused by the ruckus and the crowd.

When we finally stepped into the Doctor's clinic, it was a contrast to the world outside. I was struck by the silent, clean environment. There was an odd smell like a medicine. A woman asked me my name and many more questions while she kept writing on a large sheet. Then I was sent into a room where a man in a white coat, peered into my eyes from behind a machine. Finally, we were made to wait in a hall outside with a lot of other people for the big eye doctor to see us. After a long wait, when our turn came, we were shown into a warm room which I immediately liked. There was an elderly man with white hair and a white coat, sitting on one side of the table and he asked me to sit on the stool next to him. He examined my eyes and looked at the report on his table. Then he explained to Baba in very simple language that I had an eye disease that would get worse till I became totally blind. There was an operation, something called corneal transplant, which could help but it was expensive and not easy.

After we walked out of the clinic, Baba stopped by a tea-stall to buy me some biscuits. We hadn't had anything to eat, and I was hungry. But he didn't give it to me immediately. He said as he led us to the huge bus terminal nearby, "Be a good girl Moni, and you can have the whole packet!"

By now it was almost noon, and the sun was harsh. I could hear the buses honking and driving past. Baba took me to the benches in a waiting area and made me sit. Then he handed me the biscuits and said, "Wait here and eat these. We need to buy some things. We will finish quickly and come and get you."

I hungrily opened the packet and relished the taste of the first bite. The initial three-four I ate immediately. Then I thought I would save some for my little brother and maybe one for my older sister. There were still six left-over. I slowly nibbled on the next one and waited for Baba and Amma to return.

I waited and I waited, and I waited.

GLOSSARY

Baba – Dad
Amma – Mom
Sa'ab / Sahib ji - a respectful term for the employer or boss
Bada Sa'ab – Big Boss

Treasured

The month was May and summer was peaking. Not surprisingly, even early in the day, the heat in the kitchen was stifling. This ancient-looking room, situated in one corner of the grand Haveli, had been haphazardly modernized in patches. It had a small wooden window, with prison-like iron bars on it, which opened into the backyard, and one could see part of a huge Neem tree framed in it.

In its sooty interiors, Sashi, the queen in this part of the house, was busy preparing coconut laddoos* for Rakesh. As she lovingly shaped the sweets in the crook of her palms, she was hardly aware of the beads of sweat dotting her forehead. Blessed with flawless skin and sharp features, Shashi still had a youthful look about her. She certainly did not look like the mother of a twenty-two-year-old. Her son, for whom she was so painstakingly cooking, was returning home for his summer break from an Engineering college in the city. She had woken up early to ready her house to receive her only child. Shashi dearly missed not having him around. She hardly ever stepped into his room in his absence because she couldn't bear the emptiness. His trips home was when she came alive. She looked forward and waited for these joyful interludes in her mundane life. Not quite able to contain her excitement now, she craned her neck to look at the antique clock hanging in the hallway for the umpteenth time and called out to the family retainer,

"Kalua, have you finished doing Chhota Sa'ab's* room? He'll be here within an hour."

"Ji Bahuji*," Kalua deferentially replied.

"Have you cleaned the adjoining guest room for two of his friends who are also coming? You know how upset he gets when things are not to his liking. Also, check if the maali* has put fresh flowers in the pot."

"Don't worry bahu ji*," soothed the old man, "everything is in order."

Kalua had been with the family ever since he was a child. His father had served the family before him. Rakesh had frolicked and had grown up in his arms. He knew that the boy was the apple of his mother's eyes.

"Shanti," Shashi then turned to the cook, "don't overcook the chicken, and serve the parathas hot. The poor boy doesn't get to eat good food in his hostel. I'll go and change now. Thakur Sa'ab must be on his way back from his morning rounds of the estate."

Packing the last of the laddoos in an airtight steel jar, Shashi retrieved the silver key chain hanging at her slim waist. Despite all her excitement, as she put away the jar in the larder and locked the door, she had a feeling in the pit of her stomach that all was not well.

Tall grass grew on both sides of the railway track – wild, unruly, and swaying freely in the suction created by the moving train. Rakesh watched the scene moodily through the carriage window. He had to arrange for ninety thousand rupees within a day. The money-lender, who he had borrowed from, might get in touch with his father and then he would have had it. As it were, his results were not going to be anywhere near the expectations of the old man. Labour and drudge, that's all that he was entitled to, brooded Rakesh. A boy, a Thakur at that, was born to live like a king. He couldn't stoop to the level of a commoner now, could he, he reasoned with himself. The thought of a perfect home-made meal, a clean bedroom, and servants to do his bidding, did lift his spirits somewhat but could not put him in good cheer. He urgently needed the money to shut up that devil of a money lender or else there'll be hell to pay.

He could ask his mother as he had done earlier. He knew her ways well. She would refuse at first, then relent and give him whatever was there in her safe keeping. The price he would have to pay would be a lot of advice and harmless scolding on his wayward ways which he could ignore. But he knew that this time she would be of little help because she never would have this big an amount of cash. The old man gave her just enough for the house expenses. Alternatively, he could again try to filch a piece of her innumerable jewellery, as he had done earlier, and sell it off. But he knew she was now very careful and mindful of her keys. Of course, the last time that he had stolen her heavy bangle, a servant had been blamed and thrown out. He hadn't suffered any pangs of conscience as he had sold off the bangle in the 'chor'* bazaar. The jewellery was of little use to his mother, whereas he had hundreds of urgent needs that had to be fulfilled. He was desperate. Maybe, one last time, he could try outsmarting some gullible passenger. He, along with his two close friends, had gotten away with petty thefts in public places earlier.

Lost in reverie, Rakesh did not notice a young and smart man, take the side birth in the same compartment. His friends, Sanjay and Rajiv, did not miss the straight back, and the crew cut though. They were wary of these army types. The civilian dress couldn't camouflage the disciplined body language. While those two shrunk and melted to merge with the surroundings, Rakesh, oblivious, thought out a daring plan.

The train was nearing the last stop before his village. A honeymooning couple had been traveling with them and Rakesh had noticed the heavy gold jewellery that the woman had locked away in her husband's briefcase before sleeping. This briefcase was now lying on the opposite berth while the two lovebirds were busy with each other. He could easily snatch it, jump out of the train as it slowed down, and disappear in the tall grass outside. He could make his way to his village later. Nobody would suspect. Sanjay and Rajiv were good accomplices and would support him all the way. He knew he could count on them. Before he could warn the other two of his plans the train started to slow down. Impulsively, without thinking things through, emboldened by his earlier successes, Rakesh snatched the briefcase and ran towards the exit. As he was about to jump off, a sharp report of a pistol rang out.

The aroma of melted butter and pungent spices hung in the air. Kalua kept a steady supply of hot aloo-parathas* on the dining table from the kitchen. There was curd and homemade mango pickles to accompany it. Thakur Baldev Singh was finishing his breakfast when his cell phone rang. He ignored it for no living mortal had permission to disturb his mealtimes. The incessant ring clamoured for his attention until finally, he deigned to look. It was an unknown number. He took the call. The way he abruptly left the table and called out for his car alarmed Shashi who had been serving.

"Is everything all right?" She called after his retreating back and then muttered, "Why should I be told anything? I'm only a woman after all!"

The car slowly picked up speed on the village road amidst the dust, the animals, and the squalor. The senior Thakur sat stonily in the back seat. The ignominy of it! He hoped it was a case of mistaken identity. But deep inside of him the horror of what was to befall his prestigious family name was gripping and twisting his entails. It was his wife's fault. She had spoilt their son with her unrestricted love. Time and again he had warned her not to pamper Rakesh so much and now it had come to this.

After what seemed like ages the car finally came to a stop outside the railway station. He felt the eyes of the throng, collectively staring, and stiffened. The local sub-inspector approached him reverently and made way for him.

"This way Thakur Sa'ab," ushered the Inspector as he led him towards the platform.

As the crowd silently parted to make way, Baldev saw the body. It was lying unceremoniously dumped on a baggage trolley. It was not even covered. Thieves and robbers didn't deserve any respect. Not even in death. When he came closer, he could smell the blood and see the flies hovering. If one was looking closely at the Thakur, one would have noticed the clenching of the jaw and the throbbing pulse at the temple. But apparently, he seemed absolutely in control as he stood looking down at the body. The mop of fashioned hair on the forehead was matted with blood. The bullet had gone through the head. His eyes took it all in. The thin torso, the tall frame, the sharp nose, much like his own, and the mother's fair complexion. He turned to the Inspector brusquely and said,

"I don't know him."

GLOSSARY

Laddoos – a round sweet
Chhota Sa'ab – Young master
Ji Bahuji – Yes daughter-in-law – a respectful address
Maali – gardener
Chor – Thief
Aloo-parathas – Bread with potato filling

Escape

Winter had set in. It lay displayed in the smog which was heavy and dense. The freshly pruned trees, lining the sides of the road like sentinels, were shrouded in white. It was hardly cold in Noida, but Sneha clutched her cotton stole to her body as she tried to keep pace with her mother and two sisters. They were headed to a local housing society for their daily work. Her stomach felt knotted, and her heart raced. None of it reflected on her face though. Sharp featured, dark-skinned, with thick and long dark hair, and a lithe, tall body, she could have been picked up as a model had fate provided a better opportunity. Barely sixteen, she had been pulled out of school two years earlier because the school was far from their hutments and her mother worried about her safety. Plus, her father had far more important things to spend the meagre earnings that her mother and sisters brought home. Nowadays her income too was being used by him for drinking and gambling. Sneha had loved the school and especially the afternoon meals. Instead, she worked for a newly wedded couple as domestic help. She dreamed of a similar life of married bliss for herself.

Sneha did her best to act normal today. Her plans were well in place. A gold chain, a pair of earrings, her silver anklet – all saved by her mother for her wedding - and some savings from her earnings, were safely tucked inside her shalwar* folds. The regular drunken brawls of her father had become unbearable. She wanted a better life for herself. She was no less than any Aishwarya or Deepika adorning the posters advertising films. At least that's what Sunil told her. She smiled to herself as she thought of him waiting for her now. He had gifted her a phone which she kept well hidden.

Last night, on the pretext of going to the only toilet that ten families, living in the shanties, shared, she had finalized her escape.

"My Rani*," he had endearingly addressed her, "I can't sleep. Tomorrow, by this time, I'll be holding you in my arms."

Sneha had coyly retorted, "Shut up", but her heart had danced.

"Be near the tower at eight. I'll meet you there." She confirmed.

"Yes, Ranga, my friend, will also be there with his bike."

"Hmm, you've told me that, but have you planned where we'll go?" Sneha anxiously enquired.

"You don't worry about it. I have my friends. Everything is worked out. You just come."

"I better go now," Sneha had looked around as she said that. If her father or her younger brothers found her, she would be beaten black and blue.

Sunil blew her a kiss and said, "I love you", in a very filmy style.

As Sneha had switched off and hid the phone in her roughly stitched shalwar* pocket, she had felt elated with the idea of her perfect life with Sunil.

Once the domestic helps reached the apartment gates, their entry was marked in a register by the guard on duty. Sneha walked inside, and turned towards the flats on the right as she informed her mother,

"I'll see you all at lunch, near the garden bench, as usual."

She had no intentions of doing so. Then she pretended to go into the flat. She waited for a while under the staircase for the others to disappear. After some time she came out and furtively walked to the boundary on the opposite side of the gate. The dense thicket of trees, cloaked in fog, made a perfect setting for a getaway. She had already practised climbing one of those trees. Now she expertly climbed it, her shalwar* hitched up, and reached the top of the six feet high wall in a few seconds. The fence had barbed wires to keep intruders out. She carefully negotiated it as she looked around for Sunil. She saw a motorbike on the road with two people on it. On seeing her, the boy at the back waved. Without thinking much, Sneha jumped, aiming for the bundle of grass lying on the ground. Her shawl caught in the wire as she tumbled forward. There was no way to retrieve it, so she left it hanging there as she limped her way to the bike. Hurt but otherwise intact, she fled the scene with her beloved and his friend.

When Sneha didn't show up for work, her employer called the guard room to enquire if she had come. They confirmed her entry. Puzzled, he told his wife. She had the mobile number of the lady who employed Sneha's mother, Rukmini. So, she called her up and requested if she could speak to Rukmini. Rukmini insisted that she had seen Sneha enter the flat building. The employers maintained that she hadn't come in at all. The question then was, "Where was Sneha?"

The distraught Rukmini went around the flats looking for her daughter. The guards were questioned, and they were sure she hadn't left the premises. Was she hiding? But there was no plausible reason for her to do that. She was happy working for the couple. Had somebody forcefully taken her to their flat and were keeping her captive there? It was a remote possibility, but it couldn't be ruled out.

So, all the ten guards on duty went around questioning the flat owners. The gossip mongers went into an overdrive. Soon everyone knew that a sixteen-year-old house help had gone missing.

The forty-plus mother, with a thin body frame and a care-worn face, collected her two older daughters from the houses they worked in and rushed home. The shawl had been discovered. Rukmini feared the reaction of Sneha's father. She knew in her heart who Sneha had run away with. She had caught Sneha talking to the good-for-nothing Sunil a couple of times. That boy was a loafer who didn't do a penny's worth of work and was seen hanging around with the other village idlers, chewing tobacco. Rukmini had scolded Sneha and had warned that she would tell her father if she caught her again. Sneha seemed to have stopped but Rukmini had known that something was on. She had chosen to ignore for she hadn't foreseen the matter would take such a serious turn. Now she quaked inside as she anticipated the wrath of her husband and his two younger brothers. Sneha had put the family's honour at stake.

In the cluster of small hutments, surrounded by tall commercial buildings and modern housing apartments, a remnant of what the villages used to be like, remained. Sneha's father was waiting inside the small tenement that they lived in on rent. His huge frame filled it. He had already heard of his daughter's elopement on his cell phone from one of the apartment guards who he knew. He was fuming and his face was red. The bushy eyebrows were pulled together in a ferocious frown. The thin lips were frothing in anger.

"You slut," he hissed at his wife, "this is all your fault."

Rukmini swallowed her retort. She didn't want to aggravate him further. The girl wouldn't have gone far. If they could catch her and bring her back in time, they could still salvage the situation.

"How could I have known," she protested mildly, as tears welled up in her eyes. "Do something," she urged her husband. "Find her quickly."

"You and your daughters go whoring around and I have to run and fix all the mistakes." He shouted as he left the house in a rage.

Ravinder belonged to a small farming family from Nawari, a nearby village. The tiny piece of land that they had owned had been acquired by the government to develop the city borders. The compensation money had been substantial, but it had been divided among the three brothers and their widowed mother and it was all gone now. They still owned the small ancestral farmhouse in the village where his mother and brothers lived.

"How dare she do this to me? My dignity has been sullied forever." He fumed, as he sped on his motorbike, towards his village to seek the help of his brothers. Sneha's defiance was choking him. The humiliation of facing other men, with this blot on his name, fuelled his fury. His family's pride was at stake. It had to be restored.

"Rukmini was responsible. It was her idea to move to the city." He conveniently shifted the blame to his wife. He rarely acknowledged the fact that had they not moved when they did, the family of seven would have starved to death. He was too proud to look for work for himself. Untrained and illiterate, he didn't have many choices. Menial work, to him, was demeaning to the memory of his father who had employed casual labour to work on their farm when he was a child.

In the meantime, Rukmini asked around and found the whereabouts of the boy. She hurried alone towards a nearby Mohalla*, where Sunil's mother lived. These dwellings were worse than the area where Rukmini stayed. There was slush and squalor all around as Rukmini scrunched up her nose at the stench. Sunil's mother, she discovered, was a single woman who had been abandoned by her husband at a young age. She turned out to be an unassuming woman who was clueless about her son's activities. They seemed to be very poor by even Rukmini's modest standards.

"She couldn't have wed her daughter to this life." Rukmini reflected sadly as she made her way back. She anxiously waited for news from her husband.

Three days later, the young couple sat sipping tea on their balcony when the man exclaimed to his wife,

"Oh God, hear this," as he started to read from the newspaper he was holding.

"The body of a sixteen-year-old girl, Sneha, was discovered in the fields near Nawari yesterday with the jugular sliced at the neck. The police are on the lookout for a boy who had allegedly kidnapped the minor girl. His mother has been put under surveillance. The two uncles of the murdered girl were also interrogated."

His young wife looked at him, aghast, her eyes brimming with tears. She couldn't bring herself to believe that it was the same Sneha – so full of life and plans for her future. So curious about everything. So eager to learn. Sneha was such a common name. It could be someone else. Also, she reasoned, the mother didn't seem as upset as she should have been. She recalled that Rukmini had asked them for a loan of fifty thousand which she claimed the police had demanded for investigating further. They had not given her the money because bribing the police, to do the work they were meant to do, was dishonest and had to be discouraged. Now, they wondered if it was the price for silence.

Rukmini was working for them now in place of her daughter. She went about, doing her chores, but her eyes carried a faraway, lost look. Upon being mildly probed, she looked away and said that her husband had filed a case and the police were looking for Sneha.

The truth was sacrificed at the altar of name and honour. Dharmendra and Jitendra, the two brothers of Ravindra, had restored the family dignity, at the behest of their mother. Now they only had to lie low for a while. The local police sympathized with them. The girl had sullied herself forever. They understood the meaning of family honour. Ravindra had borrowed a hefty sum from a lender to smother any further inquiry.

Life went on as before. Rukmini didn't even have the luxury of grieving for her child. She pretended that Sneha would return one day. She blamed herself. She should have been more vigilant.

GLOSSARY

Shalwar – loose pants
Rani – Queen
Mohalla – a housing community

Goodbyes

It was a fragile silence. The whirring of the fans, an occasional turning of the paper or a shuffling of position would interrupt the uneasy quiet. Rows upon rows of students were busy pouring hastily acquired knowledge onto their examination answer sheets. With the windows closed, the heat inside the room was oppressive. Outside the sun burnt mercilessly. Aarti walked along the rows, her eyes on her students but her mind far away.

It seemed like only yesterday that her son, Aman, had been a little boy, demanding all her attention. She smiled as she recalled his habit of burying his face in the palm of her hands whenever she was annoyed or when he wanted an immediate response. When had he grown so much? There was a vast, empty space inside of her. That is where her heart should have been. Last evening, Aman had left for Australia to study Marine Engineering. Aarti had smilingly hugged her son and bid him farewell. She hated public displays of emotion and had therefore shed no tears. She had watched with a mother's pride as her handsome eighteen-year-old son had walked away towards the entrance of the airport in casuals with his laptop slung over his shoulder. The self-assurance in his poise gave her a lot of strength. She kept standing and staring long after he could be seen no more. Then she turned around to walk to her car. Her loneliness suddenly gripped her insides. Feeling numb, Aarti started her car and braced herself for a life of isolation.

It had not always been like this. Her husband, Deepak, a dynamic young officer in the country's administrative service, had filled her days with joy and sunshine. They had met and fallen in love when they were both in college. Aarti was an undergrad student of English literature while Deepak was completing his master's in economics. It was a case of opposites attracting. Aarti was sober, serious, and sincere. Deepak was full of fun, frolic, and laughter. How he loved to tease her. Tall and athletic, it was difficult not to be bowled over for even someone as grounded and sensible as Aarti. Most of the other girls in class were already dreamy eyed about him.

Deepak topped his batch and after his Masters, was offered a teaching position by the University. He accepted the offer and once secure with a job, he immediately proposed to Aarti. She was only too eager to accept. Her parents, however, were not too happy with her choice. They had hoped for somebody in a better profession, with more money, more influence. Little did they know that in two years Deepak would go on to ace the prestigious Indian Civil Services entrance exam and opt for the Administrative Service. They did not oppose the wedding though when they saw the seriousness of Aarti's attachment.

The memory of those heady, fun-filled times lifted Aarti's spirits. These recollections were the source of her strength. She went back to those days, again and again, whenever she felt the need to revive her sagging spirits. They had had such a good time together in the small apartment that they lived in during the period that Deepak was teaching at the University, and she was completing her post-graduation. Then there was the period when Deepak forgot the world to prepare for the Civil Services entrance examination. The exhilaration that followed his unprecedented success was well worth the labour of the earlier months. Then a period of training for Deepak in Mussoorie, during which Aarti did her research for an MPhil degree. A beautiful phase of her pregnancy and Aman's birth followed during the first year of Deepak's posting as a young officer. All these were treasured memories.

But inevitably, the memory of the happy times would lead her to the day when her world came crashing down around her.

Deepak was posted as the District Magistrate in a small town in Bihar. Situated in hilly terrain, it was surrounded by luxurious green jungles. Aarti, always a nature enthusiast, would often accompany Deepak on his tours to the far-flung villages within his district. She liked interacting with the tribal women and children. Someday, she hoped to write a book on them.

While returning from one such excursion, on a particularly wet and rainy day, the driver suddenly slowed down and turned to look at Deepak, sitting in the back seat with Aarti and Aman, in alarm.

"Sir," he said, "There is a crowd ahead. Looks like Maoists. What should I do?"

All of them peered through the rain. Sure enough, the road seemed to be blocked by a group of people. It was an isolated stretch with thick jungle on either side. They really didn't have a choice. It was getting late and reversing would mean going back to a place where there was no place to stay for the night. Deepak gently replied,

"I don't think they mean any harm. Drive ahead, I'll talk to them."

As the car approached the crowd, the occupants failed to notice that some of the men had heavy wooden bamboo sticks in their hands.

The driver stopped the car as the road was totally blocked. Aarti had misgivings about Deepak stepping out of the car. But Deepak authoritatively questioned the mob,

"What's all this? Why have you blocked the road?"

None answered. There was an ominous silence. Before anyone realized what was happening, a shout went up, "He's the one! He's the one!"

All hell seemed to break loose as the men started to rain their 'lathis'* on the car and on Deepak. Aman, who had been dosing in Aarti's lap, woke up shrieking. More men appeared from the surrounding jungles. Aarti started to scream at the men to stop and pushed Aman to one side as she struggled to get out of the car. They didn't allow her to open the car door initially. When she finally managed to step out, she found the crowd dissipating and then disappearing into the thickets. A police jeep had appeared from the other side and in its headlight, she saw the bloodied body of her husband on the muddy road. She ran towards Deepak as the men in uniform also scrambled to go where he was lying supine. But they were all too late. Deepak had already succumbed to grievous head injuries.

After that, it was all a blur of activities. The ambulance, the doctors, the reporters, the politicians, the relatives and finally the funeral. She survived those days in a state of semi-consciousness. She felt dead within. Sleep, thirst, hunger - all eluded her. She pretended to be alive. She felt dead from within. For the sake of Aman, she had to take hold of herself. She continued the formalities of living. She ate, dressed, and did her chores. She played with her kid and looked after his needs. But in the silence of the night, she cried her heart out. Her body craved to be held close. There was no one to share her loneliness with. Or her rage.

Officials gave her a lot of assurances of justice. Deepak had died for no fault of his. The tribal's had lashed out their anger against the government for taking over part of the jungle and turning it into a protected National Park. They had heard rumours that they will have to evacuate. Deepak was the face of the government to them. Though he had been promoting a lot of self-help employment schemes and was doing everything he could for their betterment, the rustics held him guilty for all their travails. He knew of the danger. He should not have risked his life. They were angry and he happened to be there. These were the banalities offered. It was all very simple for everyone. Since no one was caught for the murder, the injustice smouldered in her heart.

Aarti couldn't make sense of this cruel twist of destiny. Overnight her world changed. All colours seemed to have disappeared from her life. She dressed mostly in white, as was the custom for a widow. She avoided parties, especially weddings, where her presence was seen as inauspicious. She felt dead inside. Life seemed meaningless.

When she was offered an Assistant Professor's post in a government college in Patna, she accepted it. At least her days would have a purpose. Also, she had a child to look after. She gradually began to like her work. As Aman grew, her life fell into the routine of caring for the affectionate little boy and looking after her duties in the college. Her wound healed slowly and with time the searing pain, every time she was reminded of Deepak, changed into a mild longing, deep within, for something that she could never have.

Today, she had bid her son farewell. Now all that was left to Aarti was her work.

"Women should pay attention to their careers," she reflected wryly, "that is the only thing that doesn't say goodbye."

GLOSSARY

Lathi – strong bamboo stick

Voiceless

I cannot see. My eyes have not formed yet. Nor can I smell. But I can hear. My first conscious sound is the rhythmic thud thud of my mother's heartbeat. It is a source of great comfort. It lulls me to sleep and greets me on waking up. I hear other noises too. They are muffled but I can recognize them. I love my mother's voice. It is soft and sweet and almost like music. She is a good singer. Her humming I especially look forward to. I wish she would sing more often. But most of the time she seems anxious and worried. I can feel the anxiety. It makes me restless too.

I would like to see the faces behind the voices that I recognise. There is a heavy and gruff voice to which I feel very drawn. There is love and pride in that voice when it comes close to me. Mom says he is Dad. I love him almost as much as Mom. She calms down in his presence. When he is playful, Mom is her contented self. That makes me joyful too. We make a nice family – the three of us – close, comfortable, and complete.

There are other voices as well. One of them makes my mom unhappy. There is authority in that voice. Mom calls her 'Ma'. She is Dad's mother. Now Ma is very particular about what Mom eats and drinks. The other day she shouted when she caught Mom drinking a Coke. I hate loud noises. They scare me. She keeps handing Mom vegetable juices to drink. It makes her puke. She can't stand the taste. Ma tells her that it is good for me. That makes me feel awful for Mom. I don't want her to suffer on my account. Ma keeps giving a lot of advice. She talks non-stop. Mom resents it. She doesn't say anything, but I know. I am a part of her. I can feel what she feels. I laugh with her, and I cry with her.

Then there is an older voice much like my dad's. Mom calls him 'Baba'. I know he is my Dad's Dad. He doesn't talk much. I hardly hear him. But when he speaks everyone pays attention. Every day, Mom carries his morning tea to him, and he blesses her with the words,

"Dudho nahao, puto phalo." *

Though I don't understand what it means it sounds good. I like him. Dad says the news of my arrival has made him very happy. That Baba is looking forward to his first grandson playing in his lap. I would like that too. I would like to carry his tea to him one day and receive his blessings.

I want to see the faces of all these people that I hear. My eyes are slowly developing. I can see diffused light around me as I float in my haven. There is a lot of talk about my birth. It scares me to think of leaving the cosy comfort of my mother's womb. What is the world outside like? I suppose I shouldn't worry. There are so many people out there to love me and care for me.

Dad says he wants me to look like my mom because she is so pretty. Mom wants me to look like Dad because she loves him so much. Ma also wants me to look like Dad because he is so dear to her. I would like to know what I look like too. I don't much care exactly who because I can't take sides. But one thing I really want is a voice like my mom's. I would love to sing. In fact, I try to hum with my mom. I wonder if she can feel me humming. I will make her proud one day with my singing.

The day of my birth is getting closer. I can feel myself growing stronger. I am also getting more independent. It amuses me when I startle Mom with my movements. When I shift around or stretch, she gets excited and tries to feel me. When she puts her hand on her swollen belly I try to reach out and touch it. I look forward to being held in her arms.

Mom seems to be more tired these days. She probably finds it difficult to move around with so much additional weight. I would like to relieve her of the burden. But I still need to grow to be able to survive on my own.

There has been a lot of talk about a baby boy lately. My Mom says whether a boy or a girl she only wants the baby to be healthy. I think I'm healthy. I feel very healthy. But I don't know if I am a boy or a girl. I am me. But I hope I am a boy because Ma wants the firstborn to be a boy. Baba and Dad have been silent. Whatever this issue is, I want it settled because it upsets Mom. She cries later in her room. I hate that.

The issue refuses to die down. It erupts again over breakfast one day. Dad wants Mom to see a special doctor. She will tell them for sure if I am a boy or not. I am confused. What do I feel like - a boy or a girl? I feel like a little human. Will that change if I am declared a boy or a girl? I don't think so.

Mom starts to cry. She doesn't want to go. Ma shouts at her. It was something about the family name and lineage. These concepts are beyond me. Dad tries to reason out things and persuade her gently.

I dislike being the cause of so much distress. Then Baba interrupts. He calmly asks Dad to take Mom to the Ultra sonographer. That is a big and impressive word. All the noise and strife are making me uneasy. I pull my knees in and suck on my thumb.

Mom is in shock. I can feel it in her silence. Her blood has turned cold. I wonder why she is so scared of this doctor. She has been seeing doctors. Can this one be so very different?

The fear in Mom's blood stays with her, and me, the next day as she is driven to this far away clinic by Dad. I enjoy the rhythm of a car ride. It lulls me to sleep. Mom doesn't let me relax though. Her fretting makes me restless. I feel tired. I have not moved for fear of causing more distress. I feel cramped. I wish she would calm down.

Dad too doesn't talk much. He seems to be apologetic. He says he is sorry, but he must follow his parents' wishes. He cannot disappoint them. I think that is very reasonable. I will also follow his wishes and make him happy one day. But why is Mom so agitated? Should I be worried too?

The journey seems to be taking forever. Dad stops a couple of times to ask for directions. There seems to be a lot of traffic. There are blaring sounds from all around. Dad has slowed down, and I can hear him cursing. He finally stops the car and helps Mom out. I can hear car honks, tinkling of cycle rickshaws, the revving engines of auto-rickshaws, people shouting. We finally get past the din into a building.

The clinic has a bad stench. Mom sits uncomfortably on a small chair. I feel so stiff. We wait for our turn. The atmosphere is not cheerful like the other clinics that we have been to earlier. It is dark. The lighting is poor. I don't like it in here. Neither does Mom.

We are finally ushered into a small room. It has a bed on which Mom lies down. I can stretch at last. I feel sleepy. It has been a long journey. As I begin to drift off, I hear the Doctor say that the foetus is a girl. Oh no, I think, Ma will be upset. I am not prepared for my mom's reaction. She clutches her exposed abdomen and starts to weep inconsolably.

The Doctor leaves the three of us alone. She has told Dad to take a decision in five minutes. If they want to go ahead Dad must deposit a fee and get Mom admitted. Mom keeps on crying. Dad is trying to persuade her. They don't have a choice he says. Firstborn's, in their family, must be a boy. This girl can come later. I am puzzled. What does he want? Not me? This is a new feeling. Not being wanted. What have I done? I want him so desperately to love me. Mom loves me. I am sure of that. Her love is my only support in a world unknown to me.

Mom has been given an injection. She is calming down. I too am getting drowsy. A needle has appeared beside me. The water is getting salty. I squirm. I cry. This is painful. It stings. Stop it. Please.

GLOSSARY

"Dudho nahao, puto phalo" – Bathe in milk, bear sons

Entangled

The jungle - thick, unruly, and eerily dark - rushed past on either side as the old Morris forged ahead on the winding road. I was almost asleep, cosily snuggled between my mom and Grandma, on the back seat. Dad was driving with Grandpa sitting beside him in the passenger's seat. We were returning from a family wedding in a nearby town. It was late in the night. The hilly terrain, covered with a lush tropical forest, was spookily deserted. Travelling, at this hour, through these parts, was not a wise idea. The ladies, dressed and decorated like a Christmas tree, had not been happy with the decision. However, for want of a decent accommodation, plus, the lure of sleeping in their own beds, the men had decided to risk it. Grandpa, the great hunter, had his licensed revolver with him and had argued that it was only a two-hour journey. No one dared defy him.

So, here we were. One and a half hours into the journey with only a little more of the jungle left to cross when the sudden break in speed and Dad's anxious voice jolted me awake.

"Isn't that Mr Kumar's car?" He exclaimed as he braked and reversed a bit to focus the car's headlight on a clearing in the thick undergrowth.

"Strange that it should be here at this hour," responded Grandpa as he peered into the dark.

So, did all of us. I craned to see the car, a red Fiat, parked amidst the trees, almost at the edge of a steep drop. It was barely noticeable from the road. That Dad had spotted it at all was surprising. In a small town in Bihar in the sixties, the number of car owners was limited enough for people to recognize the ownership without much doubt.

"There doesn't seem to be anyone around," Dad exclaimed, after peering and honking for a while. He was preparing to shut the engine and get out to look when grandma warned from the back seat,

"Don't go out Naveen. It's not safe."

"She's right," added grandpa. "The car must've broken down and they've left it here. Someone will come back for it in the daylight I suppose. Let's go."

Dad, I could tell, wanted to explore but he couldn't defy the logic in his parent's arguments and gave in. Much to our relief, he turned on the ignition, and we were on our way. The incident was soon forgotten in the routine of day-to-day existence.

Dad, as the chief medical officer of the hilly district, was a busy man. His hospital was the only Government medical centre catering to the needs of thousands of tribal people. Mom, all the time, had a house full of family, relatives, and friends to take care of. I had my school and myriad other activities to stuff my days with. Then there were Grandma and Grandpa to pamper and dote on me. It was an idyllic existence – peaceful and happy. Little inkling did we have of the dark clouds looming on the horizon.

About a week – ten days after our return from the wedding, the town was agog with a rumour. The daughter of Mr Chandra, the 'haveli wale', was missing from her home. I knew Ruby didi*, but not too well. The few times that I had seen her had been in her own house when we had gone visiting. Though I didn't know her well, I liked her.

I remembered the first time when we had gone to Chandra Uncle's house for a Diwali party. I had been feeling lost and bored among the adult crowd when Ruby di had caught hold of my hand and had taken me around to show the lighted lamps and beautiful flower-rangoli that she had made. Hers was a gentle presence, much like that of a deer in the forest. In her early twenties, she was small and slim, with a thin face and large black eyes. She spoke sparingly and I wondered why she wore no make-up and was dressed in an all-white drab cotton sari for a party. Later, when I asked Gran, I came to know that it was the norm for a widow to dress that way.

Where could she have gone? The puzzle of her missing from home bothered me. She was such a benign person – like a piece of furniture. What could have happened? There were rumours that she may have been kidnapped for money. Her father and brother were the richest landowners of the town. The police were looking for her. Those kind, gentle eyes worried me when I was in bed, trying to sleep. I prayed for her to be home soon.

Days passed with no news of Ruby di. Then one day, our house-help told Mom that her cousin, whose husband worked as a gardener in Ruby's house, had said that Ruby had an affair with their driver's son and may have eloped with him. Though Mom shut her up, to discourage her from gossiping, she couldn't stop herself from sharing this juicy bit of news with Dad when he returned from the hospital.

They were having their evening tea in the garden. As soon as Dad heard her, he exclaimed,

"By God! Why didn't I think of this before?"

Mom looked up from the tea that she was pouring, baffled, "Think of what?" She asked.

"Chandni, do you remember seeing Chandra Kumar's car in the jungle that night?" Dad patiently reminded her, "I'm sure it has something to do with Ruby's disappearance."

I was playing within earshot, and I could hear every word of what was being said.

"What do you mean?" Mom responded in horror.

"I suspect she's been murdered!" he exclaimed dramatically.

"Who by?" Mom sounded incredulous. I was horror-struck.

"By the family," said Dad. "They are a conservative lot. They wouldn't allow a daughter of the house to have an affair outside of their caste. That too a widowed one."

"Oh my God, Naveen, you shouldn't even be saying that." My timid mother admonished as she turned pale with fear. She saw me listening and shooed me away.

Later, the four elders sat huddled together in Grandpa's room till late in the evening. Much as I would have liked to join them, I was asked to go to my room and play. The atmosphere was sombre. I was very restive. Had Ruby di been killed just because she loved someone, not of her caste? What was caste anyway? Would Dad do the same to me if I ...? Hundreds of such questions filled my eleven-year-old head. I crept out and stood quietly outside the door of Grandpa's room.

"Let's just tell the police," Grandpa was saying.

"It's none of our business," argued Grandma. "They're powerful people. Why make enemies of them?"

"Because it's the right thing to do," replied Dad.

I tiptoed back to my room. I didn't want to be discovered eavesdropping.

Early, the next morning, both the men, dressed formally, grimly drove out in the car. I knew they had gone to the police. And that was to end our cheerful, serene existence.

It was soon all over the local papers. The dailies carried front page news of the dead woman's body being found from deep in the jungle. It carried a black and white picture of the dug-up corpse. The thin frame of the woman was covered with a white sheet. There was another picture of Chandra Uncle and his son, in handcuffs, being led to the police jeep. Our family were the only witness.

It was as if the whole town woke up and was rejuvenated by this news. Everyone wanted the latest updates. Our home phone never stopped ringing. There were visitors. Lots of them. And each one needed to hear the story first-hand. We had reporters in our front lawn, taking pictures and clamouring for interviews. The policemen also kept wandering in at all times, questioning, writing, or just hanging around.

I became an overnight celebrity in my school. All my friends wanted to know what I had seen that night. In the beginning, it all seemed very exciting. But then the threats started to come, and I was targeted. The first folded piece of paper that I found in my school bag said,

"Keep quiet or your daughter will be silenced forever."

I gave it to Dad, and he turned an angry red.

"How dare they," he muttered and then barked at me, "Who gave it to you?"

"I don't know Dad," I replied, "I found it now when I opened my bag to take my books out."

I had little inkling of the seriousness of the issue, while the adults around me went into a tizzy.

Mom didn't want me out of her sight, and I didn't want to miss school. Dad wasn't sure if the police should be told. Grandma turned to her Puja room and prayed to her deity.

Grandpa settled the matter. "Poonam will go to school," he said, "and we have to inform the police. The murderers are behind bars so someone else has send the threat. We need to know who."

Dad called up the superintendent of police and told him about the threat note. He also urged him to be discreet. Investigations were on. However, that didn't stop the onslaught of warnings that followed. There were anonymous phone calls at odd hours of the day. At times even in the middle of the night. More threatening messages came through the post. The police could neither find the perpetrators nor put a stop to their activities. All they could do was offer us round-the-clock protection. Dad accepted the offer gratefully.

On the day that the father and son were to be presented in court for a bail hearing, a crude bomb was discovered in our garden. It had to be diffused, by the policemen, in a bucket of water. This incident totally unnerved my parents. If someone could plant a bomb under the watchful eyes of the police, we really were not safe, they decided.

The options were clear. Either stick to their statement of having seen Chandra Kumar's car in the jungle and face the wrath of a ruthless enemy as the case progressed or wash their hands off the whole incident and take a transfer which was long due. Dad decided on the latter. I heard him persuading a reluctant and silent Grandpa,

"It's not worth it. We'll only endanger our lives and Poonam's future. These people are ruthless and have a long reach. The girl is dead. We can't help her. I'll say in court that it was too dark and we're not sure if it was Mr Chandra's car. The police can look for other means to prosecute."

Then he added, "I have applied for a transfer".

GLOSSARY

'Haveli wale'– the large mansion owners
Didi / di – a respectful title for an older sister

A Transaction

Dr Neera Narayan looked up from the report she was hurriedly trying to finish. Her assistant in the clinic, Deepak, peeped in after a brief knock.

"Ma'am, Mr Satish is here with his wife. Will you see them?"

Neera groaned and made a face. Not today of all days! She was trying to close as she had to be present for her daughter's sixteenth birthday party and was already running late.

"He didn't make an appointment, did he?" She asked.

"No Ma'am, but he said he'll only take a minute. Since his wife is an old patient of yours, I thought I should inform you," reasoned Deepak.

Reluctantly, Neera gave her consent, "Send them in."

She could not have ignored Satish and Shweta. This couple had been undergoing in vitro fertilization treatment for the past two years and their extreme longing for a child after thirteen years of marriage had touched her somewhere deep inside.

Satish walked in first with his air of precise control. Slim and suave, he presented a pleasing picture in his white shirt and grey blazer.

"Hello Doctor," He said breezily, "good evening."

"Ah! Good evening" Neera replied as she met the eyes of the shy Shweta walking behind her husband. Fair and willowy, with a faraway expression in her brown eyes, Shweta was a pretty woman. Today she was wearing an expensive pink chiffon sari, with sequins on the border. They made a handsome couple. Neera wondered at the vagaries of nature. Why hadn't a couple like them been blessed by a progeny?

"So, what brings you here today?" Neera asked on a cheerful note.

"Doc, tomorrow we are scheduled to try out the latest technology in IVF, the Embryo scope system. Since Shweta has so much faith in you, she insisted on seeking your blessings before we begin," informed Satish.

"That is a wise decision," encouraged Neera. "I have been asking Shweta to try it out. The average success rate of IVF for women of thirty-five years of age is about thirty per cent. The Embryo scope system greatly increases the odds. I shall keep my fingers crossed." Neera smiled as she hurriedly stood up and Shweta bent down to touch her feet.

"Hey, don't do that!" She exclaimed. "You make me feel so old." But her hand automatically moved to touch Shweta's head in blessing.

"I'm sorry I have to hurry today. There are friends waiting for me." Neera added as she made her way out of the clinic. She stopped by Deepak's desk to leave some instructions with him and asked him to close for the day.

The couple followed her to her car and Satish held her door open as she got in.

"All the best," she said.

"We'll keep you posted," replied Satish.

"Do that," Neera responded as she backed out her Sedan from the parking lot. She could see them in her rear-view mirror, waving to her as drove away.

"Let it succeed Lord," she sent a little prayer as she adjusted the mirror to look at herself. The face which looked back was pretty in a pixie sort of way. Almond eyes and a small sharp nose in a heart-shaped face. Neera pouted at herself as she applied some lipstick. Not bad, she thought, but wished she had fuller lips as she eased her car into traffic.

The next time Neera saw Shweta and Satish was about three months later when they came to her for an ultrasound. They clearly looked elated and very excited. Satish told Neera that Shweta had tested positive and finally seemed to have conceived. But they wanted Neera to do an ultrasound and make doubly sure.

As Neera squeezed jelly over Shweta's abdomen and put the probe in place, the tension in the room was palpable. She adjusted the monitor to get a clearer picture and started moving the probe. She could clearly see the gestational sac, an early sign of pregnancy.

"Congratulations dear," she beamed at Shweta, "It seems to have worked. You're pregnant!"

The two were like young adolescents in love - elated, happy, and excited. As Neera cleaned the jelly with tissues, Satish bent down to retrieve his wife's slippers. She had never seen him do that before!

She could understand this new tenderness and wished them both well.

Then they disappeared.

Neera had expected that they would come for routine Ultrasound as the pregnancy advanced. She was a busy practitioner and couldn't afford to waste much time mulling over any one individual patient's progress. But she did wonder about those two. She was concerned and would have liked to know how the pregnancy was progressing.

Months passed and Neera almost forgot about Satish and Shweta. Then, one evening, he suddenly made an appearance at her clinic, alone and unannounced.

Deepak, her secretary, was on leave and Neera was managing her patients herself. She was busy typing a report when Satish knocked and entered to her response of "yes?"

For a second, Neera couldn't place him, and then it all came back to her.

"Oh my God," she exclaimed exaggeratedly, "Look who's here!"

"Good evening, Doc," responded the perfect gentleman. "How have you been?"

"I'm great. But how are you? And where is Shweta? Isn't she here? I hope everything's fine?"

Satish smiled and said, "Yes, yes everything's fine. I've been meaning to come and see you but for most of this past year, we have been living in Bombay with my parents. Shweta needed care and my mother could look after her. We're back in Delhi now."

Neera waited for more news. She didn't want to ask what had happened to the pregnancy in case things had gone wrong. So, she probed delicately, "Oh, I see. But how is Shweta?"

"She's busy with the baby. We have a son."

"Congratulations! I'm so happy for you. Was the delivery normal?" asked an excited Neera.

"No, a caesarean; there were triplets, A boy and two girls. Three would have been unmanageable. I sold off the two girls."

"Sold off?" enquired an incredulous Neera.

"Yes Doc," said Satish, "there is quite a market and we had incurred big expenses, so we thought 'why not'?"

Neera stared at Satish. She was speechless.

Dearly Beloved

I was in an unknown place. There were thousands of people milling about but they were all strangers. Alone and in deep distress, I looked around desperately for Yusuf, my husband, but he was nowhere to be found. I didn't have money or papers and I had to find Yusuf. I woke up in a panic. Then I realised I had been dreaming. A recurrent nightmare that had no rational explanation. I brushed it away as I tried to figure out what time it was. I rarely slept so deeply during the day.

The light in the room had changed. It had turned a little chilly. The quality of the light that filtered in through the floral curtain was darker, thicker. I could hear the rumble of the rolling thunder. It was August, the month for monsoon rains. When I peeped outside, I found the sky covered by dark billowing clouds. I let the curtain slide back to its place. My heart felt as heavy and laden as the air outside. An afternoon siesta is a bad idea, I scolded myself. That the rains were beating a retreat was a consoling thought. Winter would soon be here and winter in Delhi was always beautiful.

I switched on the bedside lamp and put on a soft ghazal on the vintage gramophone that Yusuf had gifted to me as our first anniversary gift. It was one of my most prized possessions. The throaty and melodious voice of Abida Parveen crooning, "Aahat *si koi aaye to lagta hai ke tum ho...*" lifted my spirit. I called the cook to bring my tea and went out into the balcony to enjoy the sight of the misty rain on the lush green grass of my lawn. This was not the season for flowers, but the greens were flourishing. The creepers in the hanging baskets were thick and luscious. The charming Clematis, the Japanese ivy, the spider plant, the money plant – all had covered this first floor terrace to give it a very cosy, private air. I checked the seeds in the bird feeders hanging around and refilled some. This was my favourite spot in the house. If the weather permitted, I usually carried my books here.

Today, an ennui had set in. I didn't feel like reading or writing. Also switching on the lights at this hour would mean inviting a swarm of insects this way. I sat in the fading light, staring without seeing. Murli, our cook, came in with the tray and I reached out for my cup. As I took in the aroma of the pure Darjeeling tea, my eyes were drawn to the iPhone lying on the cane chair beside me. I put down the tea as I picked it up. As usual, there was a horde of messages waiting.

I lazily deleted all the junk messages. I went to my WhatsApp account and ran my eyes through the groups. Alumni school group, college batch, social circle, my family, his family, University colleagues, women's circle, music group, reading group – the list was endless. I clicked on 'my family' and smiled at the picture of the month-old baby that my niece had posted. I sipped as I scrolled. My family and my husband's clan together were huge, and I found this a quick way to keep in touch. As for my social circle, since Yusuf was a busy man and I was not very keen on partying with friends on my own, this worked as a happy middle ground. I was averse to losing touch altogether.

Now Facebook was another matter. I found it too public a platform. I rarely navigated it, but I found it useful for connecting with people I'd lost touch with and a handy birthday and anniversary reminder tool. Beyond that, the boastfulness of the posts put me off. Humility seemed to be a virtue long dead and buried. As I ran my eyes down these stories, I suddenly remembered that the birthday of a friend was coming up. She was an FB friend of my husband's, so I typed 'Yusuf Afridi' and his home page opened. He had recently changed his profile picture. With proud ownership, I enlarged the picture to take a closer look. My dashing forty-five-year-old Architect looked handsome in his denim shirt. Tall and slim, with an athletic body, he was laughing into the camera as he tried to navigate a sailboat. His thick peppered hair was blowing in the wind and contrasted attractively with his Oakley shades. The picture had been taken by me on our last vacation in Sri Lanka. I could seriously take up photography as a second profession, I thought vainly as I smiled. I was good at it.

I rarely ever visited Yusuf's FB account. There never was a need for doing so. We were constantly interacting and exchanging notes – at mealtimes, in bed, over tea, on phone. And I was a person who minded my own business and hated prying. Our relationship was based on complete trust, and I didn't believe in keeping tabs. I had opened his page perhaps once earlier. So, the large number of photographs that he had posted took me by surprise. I had not seen most of these. As I looked at them, I also read the appreciative comments made by his FB friends. I kept taking small sips of my tea. My eyes were drawn to the prominent presence of one particular woman. She was responding and interacting on every picture. I knew her. She worked in the HR department of Yusuf's firm. A blatantly seductive, provocatively dressed female who any wife would be wary of. My antenna went up. What was going on here? I wasn't aware that she was on such close terms. The more I read, the more alarmed I became. My heart started to race. I was breathing harder. My palms became sweaty as I slowly navigated through all that was there. The tea went cold.

The second shock was when I saw the status. 'Single' it proclaimed to the world. We had been happily married for over twenty years. Was it something he had overlooked maybe? I tried to make excuses. There was nothing offensive here, really. But a cold fear gripped my insides. I frantically tried to look for my name, Ayesha, or my picture. There were none. Even a dimwit would know there was something going on.

Never one to stifle emotions, I knew I wouldn't be able to ignore this. My mind went into turmoil. Talk I must, but how? An aggressive confrontation was not in my nature. At the same time, I didn't want to let it go unaddressed. Women friends of my husband had never been an issue between us. To live and let live had always been our way. Yusuf enjoyed female company and that never bothered me. But this woman from his office, this Lali Kukreja, I instinctively didn't trust. So, the next thing I did was click on her name and check out her page.

Fair, sharp-nosed, full lips, thick jawline, with a short boy cut hairstyle– she was attractive, but mannish. Her well-upholstered build was thrown to full advantage by the tightly fitted and revealing clothes that she was wearing in most of the pictures. And what pictures! One had her sticking her tongue out at the camera in a provoking pose. In another, she was showing off her backless blouse tied with two thin strings. I wouldn't be seen dead in these, I thought irritably, as I spied some more. Selfies flooded her posts. There were some pictures of her with a six-year-old daughter in pigtails. Not one photo of her husband. I remembered hearing from the office staff that her marriage was estranged.

It was late evening when Yusuf finally returned from work. The sun had gone down, and the crickets were creating a ruckus. I hadn't stirred from my chair. I had agonised myself into a deep state of anxiety. Other bits and pieces of worry had added up to create a state of turbulent unrest. We talked less, shared fewer intimacies, and his need for me had lessened. This was hugely different from how things had been earlier. He seemed to have lost all interest in sex. I had dismissed it as a natural ageing process. Little things were now bothering me. I pushed back the chair and unsteadily got up on my feet when I heard Yusuf in the bedroom.

Never onc to hide emotions, "I want to talk to you," I blurted out as soon as I saw him.

"About what?" He asked guardedly, as he started to take off his shoes.

I went and sat next to him on the bed, put my hand on his arm and softened my voice, "Don't you feel that we're moving apart? Shouldn't we discuss what's wrong?"

"Nonsense. There's nothing to discuss." He moved brusquely away.

But I wouldn't relent. My vision had blurred. My throat constricted as I appealed,

"We have to be honest *Suf.* What is going on?"

He looked alarmed but wriggled out of the situation by buying time –

"I'm in a rush now. I've to change and attend a presentation in office. There's cocktail and dinner too but I'll eat at home."

I stared at him, dumbstruck. He went into the washroom and emerged a little while later, from the walk-in wardrobe, dressed elegantly in crisp blue shirt and black trousers. I took pride in keeping his clothes and shoes in perfect order.

When he saw me still sitting on the bed, he relented and said, "Let me get back Ayesha, we'll discuss."

And then he left.

I could smell the Armani that I'd gifted him recently.

After he'd gone, I tried to distract myself with work. As a professor of English Literature, I had a lot of work to do before the week started. But I was too restive, and my mind refused to focus. As was my habit, I started cleaning the mess, left behind by Yusuf, in the dressing area of the washroom.

It wasn't unusual for Yusuf to attend these functions organised by his company. As the chief architect, he was expected to participate in all the major presentations for clients that his juniors organised.

I went downstairs into the kitchen.

"Murli, what are you making for dinner?" I asked the cook as I started looking into the pots on the stove.

"Fried peas and potatoes, chicken curry and rice," he rattled.

"Why? Can't you change the menu occasionally?"

I knew I was being unreasonable. I just had to order, and he would oblige. I tried to curb my petulance.

"Help me make a pudding. Take out the eggs and milk." And I got busy.

Yusuf returned late that night. When he came the dinner was already laid out and I was waiting. 'No arguments on the dinner table' had always been my mantra. Disturbed and tense, I affected normalcy. As we ate, Yusuf told me about the interesting presentation that evening. It had to do with a new concept for a hospital building that was coming up. Though I loved rice, I played around with the food on my plate. He asked for a second helping of the pudding that I'd baked but didn't compliment me, as he usually did.

When we were finally settled in bed, I gingerly broached the subject.

"Yusuf," he looked at me questioningly, "you had promised to tell me something, remember?"

A shadow crossed his face. He seemed to be struggling with himself.

"You have to tell me. What's bothering you?" I persisted. "How else will I ever know why you seem so distant? We are not communicating like we used to."

When he didn't respond, I went on – "You cannot keep to yourself like this. We hardly talk nowadays. Our love life has disappeared. Why?" I was warming to my subject and my anxiety came pouring out in a gush of words.

"Do tell me what it is. Are you overworked? Is there something wrong in the office? Are you feeling sick? Or you don't love me anymore?"

This was getting dramatic. I knew how much he loved me – that I was the centre of his universe. But once on to it there was no stopping. I just couldn't control myself. The question that was hovering on my tongue was "What is that woman doing on your FB page?" But I did not want to name her.

And then it came. A bolt out of the blue.

"We are in love."

"What!" Followed by an equally incredulous "Who?" My mind had shut down in shock.

He did not look at me as he continued.

"We've been in a relationship for the last five years. We've tried to stop and break off but haven't been able to. I cannot live without her."

I felt cold. My mind refused to function. I felt worse than when my father had died. Shock. Denial. Bewilderment. I went through all of it. And while my whole being tried to cope, my tongue got busy reasoning, arguing, cajoling.

"What are you saying? Are you out of your mind! You are not thinking straight. You are my husband. You are a married man. We've built such a beautiful life together. You are infatuated. This is not love. You have no idea what you're talking about. See, think about this..." I went close to him and pulled his face to look at me as I continued,

"What if I and she were caught in a fire and you could only save one of us. Who would you choose?" I was so sure he would say 'you'. I was the mother of his only son. He kept quiet.

"Tell me", I repeated, "Who would you save?"

"Both." He mumbled miserably.

"You have to choose," I insisted, trying to clear his brain. "You can only save one."

"I too will jump into the fire." He declared finally.

That did it. I totally broke down. Tears streamed down my face as I ran out of the room.

Once I was in the guest room, on the ground floor, I cried my heart out. I howled and howled. Somewhere within me lurked a hope that this man, who had never been able to handle my tears, would walk in, take me in his arms and assure me that everything would be alright. But the night passed undisturbed. I lay sprawled on the bed, alternating between sobbing brokenly and trying to sleep.

Painful memories bolted through me and seared my very being. My mind was in a state of fever. Episodes kept coming back to me in pieces. All those times when Yusuf had returned late from office. Had he really been working? There were times when I had lovingly cuddled against him, and he had moved away from me. The time when I had badly wanted to go on a holiday, and he had pretended to be over busy. The betrayal, the heartache, the 'we'- that hurt me the most. Since when had my husband and this other woman become 'we'? How did I get pushed out? I felt like walking out of the house. I felt disgusted. So, cheated.

But go where? Our eighteen-year son, Asif, was returning home from UK in two days. I had to be here for him. I couldn't tell him all this. There were two important classes, and a meeting with the principal, scheduled the next day in college. I just couldn't not show up. I had to honour my commitments. I had to be rational. I had to be sensible, I kept telling myself. Being impulsive or silly wasn't how I functioned.

My heart was bleeding. Try as much as I could, there was no consoling me. I was so upset. So distraught. Visual images of Yusuf doing things to that woman – kissing her, caressing her, making love – kept torturing me through the night.

I tried to reign in my tormented mind. I told myself this will all blow over. It was just a bad dream. I would put it right. He had always been impulsive. Passionate. I had always had to make him see sense. Through love, through logic, through persuasion, reason always prevailed. After all, he hadn't chosen her over me. He was confused. I placed my hope on his intelligence.

The next moment I was seized by panic. It was as though I couldn't breathe. Now what? How could he do this? Did all that we share, in our twenty years together, mean nothing to him? He had loved me so madly, so intensely.

"Things fall apart, the centre cannot hold"

My frenzied mind repeated the line from Yeats as I fell into an anguished sleep sometime during the night.

GLOSSARY

Aahat *si koi aaye to lagta hai ke tum ho* – any sound seems like you are approaching

Mixed Feelings

I stood undecided, with my wardrobe open, not quite sure what to wear. I wanted something formal and chic but subtle. It was my first day as an assistant professor in a government college. I wanted to look my best, but one also had to fit into a conservative set-up seamlessly. Finally, I reached out for the ethnic blue sari that I had bought from Fabindia. I held it against me as I turned around and faced Amir, my husband.

"How will this look?" I asked him.

"Great," he replied, without really looking. Then added, "You look nice in whatever you wear."

I really didn't expect him to say anything different. In our ten years of marriage, he had always supported me in whatever I chose to do.

"Will catch up in the evening," he added as he rushed to leave for his office. "Are you sure you'll find your way to this college by yourself Erum?"

"Of course, I will. I don't want you to tag along as a guardian angel." I smiled to reassure him.

"I'm concerned because you've never been to that part of the city." He clarified.

"I'll be fine, don't you worry," I reassured him as I gave a little playful push. "You get going, I need to dress."

Later, as I manoeuvred my Maruti Suzuki through the maddening Monday morning traffic, I wished I had accepted Amir's offer. At the same time, I was happy I had not. There were no rights without responsibilities, I firmly maintained, and in the process of staying responsibly independent, I often stretched myself to my limits. In the privacy of the car, I exulted at my achievement. It had not been easy. To work for a Ph D degree and qualify in the National Eligibility Test for college teachers, with two little children and a home to care for, was no mean task. I had been working in private institutions before this. Now that my daughter was also going to school along with my son, I had thought of applying for the prestigious state university service. With an impeccable academic record to my credit, selection was certain. What thrilled me was that I topped the list of candidates chosen. My hiatus from my career hadn't affected my prospects. I had reported at the university headquarters which was not too far from where we lived. But I had been posted in a member College which was in the outskirts of the city.

After stopping several times to ask for directions I finally spotted the college gates with KPS College painted on a signboard as old as the college itself. I was disappointed. It was a five storied building, badly in need of repairs. At one time it must have been painted in creamy white. Now all of it appeared a dirty yellow with patches of amoeba-shaped plaster visible where the paint had eroded. The ground in front was large with a driveway but scraps of wild vegetation had overtaken what must have been a lawn once. I cautiously drove in and parked to one side. Groups of people - students and teachers - stopped and stared as I made my way in. Later, I came to know that

I was the first woman driver to have entered the college precincts. Some feat in twenty first century India indeed!

My excitement at joining was fast turning into trepidation. I braced myself as I tried to locate the Principal's Chamber. It was not too difficult to spot. In the dingy corridor that I stepped into; one room had a crowd hanging outside it. I made my way there and looked in. A muscular, moustachioed man in a white khadi kurta and a brown Nehru jacket, sat behind an office desk. He looked more like a politician than an academic. He was surrounded by several men talking and chatting. Some were sipping tea from small paper cups. There was a plate of samosas lying on the table which was fast being devoured. I stood at the door after a brief knock, waiting to be called in.

The principal looked at me but said nothing. I was puzzled. What was expected of me?

While I stood demurely waiting, I took in the broken plaster on the walls and the shabby floor. The cobwebs on the ceiling, the curtainless windows, and the chipped door - all projected a dismal picture. True to my public-school upbringing I knocked again. A little louder this time.

"You need a special invitation?" The principal asked me sarcastically.

"Good morning, Sir," I wished as I hastily walked in.

"My name is Erum Hasan. I have come to join this college as an Assistant Professor in Economics." I hurriedly explained as I handed him my joining letter.

He briefly looked through it, signed it and passed it to one of the men in his office.

"Put it in Madam's file," he ordered and then shot a rapid-fire-round of questions at me about my qualifications and teaching experiences.

All this while I was kept standing. Not one of the men, sitting in the room, offered me a chair. The principal could have called for an extra one to be brought in, but he didn't bother. It was a demeaning experience. When he was done with interviewing, he asked me to go to the examination section. I was to be put on invigilation duty that day.

Already feeling small, I warily found my way to the examination centre on the first floor. It was a room surrounded by decrepit almirahs bursting with files and yellowing papers. There was a table in the middle on which were stacked bundles of sheets and printed papers. A few men stood around chatting. I approached them and introduced myself.

"I'm Erum Hasan. I've just joined, and the principal has asked me to report here for duty."

"Good, Madam," said one of them. "You can go to the lecture hall on the fourth floor with these examination copies and question papers. The students are already there."

There were a zillion questions in my head but before I could ask even one, I heard a voice say,

"I'll go with her."

I looked towards the voice. A man in his mid-forties, average height, ordinary looking, dressed in shirt and trousers was leaning against the dirty window and was sizing me up. I looked away, grateful for the help. By myself, I would have been at sea.

"Okay Ramavatar ji*, you go with Madam to 401," said the man-in-charge, handing us our bundle of papers.

We made our way through the shabby staircase to the fourth floor. I could smell the heavily perfumed hair oil on my fellow teacher's head. I didn't approve of it or the fact that he had his mouth full of paan*.

"What have I got myself into." I sighed and repeated the words from Bible, "Father, forgive them, for they know not what they do."

More shock was in store. The room on the fourth floor was a little too well ventilated for my taste. There were no grills or shutters on the half-dozen windows which overlooked a sleazy looking backyard, which, I later discovered, had a huge water body choked with algae and some water lilies. The wooden benches were overflowing with clamouring students. They fell silent as we walked in but soon started to chat again. I was appalled at the lack of discipline. I was thinking of bringing some order when my co-invigilator started shouting at the students - threatening, cursing, and rudely barking instructions. They fell silent and I got busy distributing the answer sheets and the question paper. I kept my disapproval to myself. This was totally unfamiliar ground, and I was in an observant mood. Maybe this is how these colleges functioned, I reasoned.

One hour into the duty, when things had settled and the only noise one could hear was the shuffling of papers and an occasional creaking of the fixed benches as the undergraduates shifted in their places, Ramavatar ji stopped by me. I was standing near a door, keeping my eyes at the examinees, to discourage them from cheating.

"So, Madam, where do you live?" He asked me casually.

"New Rajendra Colony," I replied in a low voice, careful about not disturbing the class.

"With your parents?" He wanted to know.

"No," I said, "with my husband."

"Oh!" He exclaimed, "I didn't think you were married."

I smiled back and added, "I have two children."

He looked at me from my head to my toe and said, "You don't look it!" in an incredulous tone.

I didn't like the drift of the conversation and tried to move away. He stopped me by shooting another question.

"What does your husband do?"

"He's into management," I reluctantly replied.

"Where?"

"HMT." I was trying to be civil.

"How old are your children?"

Now I wanted to ask him to mind his own business but answered, "Eight and Five."

"Boys?" He was looking at me in a way that made me uneasy.

"The older one is a boy, the younger is a girl."

Again, I tried to move away, but he blocked my way.

"What family planning method do you adopt, Madam?" He questioned with a smirk.

"What?" I was incredulous. Did this man, whom I had just met, want me to share the most intimate details of my life.

"You have maintained yourself well," he added with a grin.

Before he could say anything more, I pretended to answer a student and moved briskly to the other side of the room.

To say I was dismayed would be an understatement. I felt affronted, insulted, mortified. I didn't know what to do. I wanted to take the man to task but I held back because I didn't want to create a scene on the first day at work. All I could do was avoid the man. The day somehow got over. I felt tense and all knotted up inside as I drove back home.

When I walked in, Amir was already there. Our house help had cleaned up behind me and the house looked inviting and cosy. The kids had changed and were happily playing. I walked into our bedroom. Amir turned down the volume of the tv channel as I went to him and flopped by his side.

"How was your first day?" He brightly asked.

I looked at him and burst into tears.

"What happened?" He asked aghast.

I cried my heart out. And I kept saying, "I'm not going there anymore."

Finally, when I calmed down, I told him what had happened.

Amir calmly fetched me a glass of water. Then he reasoned with me,

"Erum, you'll find such characters everywhere. You can't quit because of them. You must learn to handle them. We'll talk about this later. Wash and change now. Let's eat."

When I woke up the next morning I felt more in control. Amir was right, I thought. I'll deal with this. With my mind made up, I wrote a detailed letter to the principal complaining of improper behaviour. Armed with my letter and a fighting spirit, I made my way to the college once again.

It took a lot of courage to walk into the principal's chamber. Thankfully I found him alone. I wished him and handed the letter.

"Sir, this is a complaint against a professor's misbehaviour yesterday."

I could see he was shocked, but he accepted the letter without saying anything. I said "thank you" before quickly exiting. I was in no mood to go into details of what had happened. My letter was self-explanatory.

By afternoon, almost everyone in the staffroom knew about the letter. Other teachers wanted to know what had happened. Some ladies were happy that I had complained. They said that Ramavatar was a habitual offender. There were some who gave me looks of disapproval. I was uncomfortable but I kept up a stoic front as I went about taking care of the duties assigned to me for the day. That man was not seen.

Early in the morning the next day I got a call from the principal's assistant.

"Erum Madam," he said, "Principal sa'ab has asked you not to come to the college."

"Why?" I questioned, shocked.

"You've been transferred for your misconduct. You will get a letter today." He abruptly hung up.

I kept looking at my phone in disbelief - angry and relieved at the same time.

Glossary

Ji – a respectful address like a title
Paan – betel quid

Author's Note

It is said that fact is stranger than fiction. This is true for this anthology of short stories which I choose to call 'Pebbles' for they are that. Little known, unheard, unsung, everyday occurrences, scattered around like pebbles. These are all true stories – either based on experience, hearsay or on newspaper headlines. They are fictionalized and woven around the lives of females. They may come across as shocking because that is the purpose – to tell the story in a way that jolts the readers out of their complacency. To draw attention to lives such as these, being lived around us, touching us, and then getting lost in oblivion. That these occurrences are real-life and from contemporary India point to the appalling state of lives that are still being lived.

Acknowledgements

I would like to acknowledge my gratefulness for this work seeing the light of the day to several kind hearts in my life…

My dear friend, Dr Neema Agrawal. The title name "Pebbles' was her idea.

My family, especially my children – Saima and Yamaan and their spouses Arzi and Nazreen respectively– for their generous help with reading, editing, and technical support.

My husband – Mohib and my mother, for always being there to support and encourage.

Mr Subi Nagpal, for the motivation, and the drive, to publish.

To my nephew, Arbab, who claims to have turned me into a storyteller, through his pestering to narrate tales to him as a kid.

Author's Profile

Professor Ghazala Naaz heads the Department of English at NIET (Noida Institute of Engineering & Technology), under APJ Abdul Kalam Technical University, Lucknow, India. She has taught English language, literature, and linguistics for over thirty years to a wide variety of tertiary level learners in several universities. She has also been involved with training in personality development and communication.

Dr Naaz's area of research is Indian writings in English and feminist criticism. She has published various articles, in International and National journals. She is also the editor of two professional journals and one newsletter of her Institute. This is her first attempt at fiction.

A mother of two, she lives in Greater Noida, with her husband, a surgeon.

9 789393 388322

Printed by Libri Plureos GmbH in Hamburg, Germany